Contemporary Chinese Poetry
in English Translation Series

Hai Zi
Selected Poems

Translated by Dan Murphy（慕浩然）

教育部人文社会科学重点研究基地
安徽师范大学中国诗学研究中心　组编
Chinese Poetry Research Center of Anhui Normal University

杨四平 主编　　上海文化出版社

当代汉诗英译丛书

海子诗歌英译选

[美] 慕浩然 译

CONTENTS

目录

FARMING PEOPLE

In bluing river water

wash both hands

wash the hands that fought in ancient battles

the group hunt, already so distant from us

doesn't now fit

my blood

take the sword

armor

and crown

bury them all in the lofty mountains that surround us

a horse cart from the north

settles into the tender affection of yellow earth

pieces of the earth passed from generation to generation

asleep in our seed bags

1983

农耕民族

在发蓝的河水里
洗洗双手
洗洗参加过古代战争的双手
围猎已是很遥远的事
不再适合
我的血
把我的宝剑
盔甲
以至王冠
都埋进四周高高的山上
北方马车
在黄土的情意中住了下来

而以后世代相传的土地
正睡在种子袋里

1983

HISTORY

The first time our lips hold
blue water
a clay jar brimming
and a dozen southern stars
tinder
the first painful separation

years...

you're the one clad in black
in the wilderness discovering the first plants
feet thrust into the earth
never to be removed
lonely flowers
are the forgotten lips of spring

years...years

历史

我们的嘴唇第一次拥有
蓝色的水
盛满陶罐
还有十几只南方的星辰
火种
最初忧伤的别离

岁月呵

你是穿黑色衣服的人
在野地里发现第一枝植物
脚插进土地
再也拔不出
那些寂寞的花朵
是春天遗失的嘴唇

岁月呵，岁月

in B.C. we are too young
in A.D. we are too old

no one knows that true and beautiful smile
but I raise my hand and knock on the door
the hieroglyphics that I carried
scattered on the ground
years...years

once at home
I slowly remove my hat
leaning on those who love me
close my eyes
an ancient bronze statue sits in the wall
bronze steeped in tears

years…

1984

公元前我们太小
公元后我们又太老

没有人见到那一次真正美丽的微笑
但我还是举手敲门
带来的象形文字
撒落一地

岁月呵
岁月

到家了
我缓缓摘下帽子
靠着爱我的人
合上眼睛
一座古老的铜像坐在墙壁中间
青铜浸透了泪水

岁月呵

1984

THE ARLES SUN*
— FOR MY EMACIATED BROTHER

"All the things I have created in nature are chestnuts snatched from the fire. Oh! Those who do not believe in the sun betray God. " **

Go south

go south

your blood, without lovers or springtime

without the moon

there isn't even enough bread

friends even scarcer

only a throng of suffering children, gobbling up everything

my emaciated brother, Van Gogh, Van Gogh

from beneath the earth vigorously spurting forth

like a volcano with no thought for the results

cypresses and wheat fields

and you

spurting forth your remaining time

阿尔的太阳 *
——给我的瘦哥哥

"一切我所向着自然创作的，是栗子，从火中取出来的。啊，那些不信仰太阳的人是背弃了神的人。"

到南方去
到南方去
你的血液里没有情人和春天
没有月亮
面包甚至都不够
朋友更少
只有一群苦痛的孩子，吞噬一切
瘦哥哥凡·高，凡·高啊
从地下强劲喷出的
火山一样不计后果的
是丝杉和麦田
还有你自己

just one of your eyes could illuminate the world

but you use your third eye, the Arles sun

to burn the starry sky into a crude river

to burn the earth into its rotation

raising your yellowed spasmodic hand, sunflowers

inviting all those who have pulled chestnuts from the fire

not to paint again Christ's olive garden

if you must paint, paint the reaping of olives

paint a violent ball of fire

to substitute for the father of heaven

washing life clean

red-haired brother, drinking up the absinthe

you light this fire

burn

1984.4

*Arles is a small town in southern France where Van Gogh created 70 or 80 paintings during the most brilliant period in his career. [Hai Zi's own footnote.]

* *The two sentences in the quote above are apparently taken from two separate letters Van Gogh wrote to his brother Theo.

喷出多余的活命时间
其实，你的一只眼睛就可以照亮世界
但你还要使用第三只眼，阿尔的太阳
把星空烧成粗糙的河流
把土地烧得旋转
举起黄色的痉挛的手，向日葵
邀请一切火中取票的人
不要再画基督的橄榄园
要画就画橄榄收获
画强暴的一团火
代替天上的老爷子
洗净生命
红头发的哥哥，喝完苦艾酒
你就开始点这把火吧
烧吧

1984.4

＊阿尔系法国南部一小镇，凡・高在此
创造了七八十幅画，这是他的黄金时期。

ME, AND THE OTHER WITNESSES

The stars and sheep herds of my hometown
like rows and rows of white, beautiful streams
running past
a small deer runs past
hunted by the gazes of the night

in the open wilderness, discovering the first plant
    feet thrust into the earth
never to be removed
lonely flowers
are the forgotten lips of spring

for our days
leave the scars on our faces
because there is nothing else to bear witness for us

me and the past

我，以及其他的证人

故乡的星和羊群
像一支支白色美丽的流水跑过
小鹿跑过
夜晚的目光紧紧追着

在空旷的野地上，发现第一枚植物脚插进土地
再也拔不出
那些寂寞的花朵
是春天遗失的嘴唇

为自己的日子
在自己的脸上留下伤口
因为没有别的一切为我们作证

separated by black earth
me and the future
separated by soundless air

I plan to sell off everything
I'll take whatever price is offered
except for tinder, the tool for fire
except for my eyes
eyes struck by you until they bled

one eye left to the scattered flowers
one eye never to leave this city's iron gates
    a black well

1984.6

我和过去
隔着黑色的土地
我和未来
隔着无声的空气

我打算卖掉一切
有人出价就行
除了火种、取火的工具
除了眼睛
被你们打得出血的眼睛

一只眼睛留给纷纷的花朵
一只眼睛永不走出铁铸的城门
　　黑井

1984.6

THE BRIDE

The small wooden homes of our hometown, chopsticks, a jar
 of clear water
and afterwards many, many days
many, many partings
illuminated by you

today
I will say nothing
let others speak
let the boatman far out on the river speak
there is a lantern
it is the river's faint eye
sparkling
tonight, it sleeps in my home

after a month when we open the door
some flowers blooming high in the trees
some fruits born deep in the ground

1984.7

新娘

故乡的小木屋、筷子、一缸清水
和以后许许多多日子
许许多多告别
被你照耀

今天
我什么也不说
让别人去说
让遥远的江上船夫去说
有一盏灯
是河流幽幽的眼睛
闪亮着
这盏灯今天睡在我的屋子里

过完了这个月，我们打开门
一些花开在高高的树上
一些果结在深深的地下

1984.7

ASIAN COPPER

Asian copper, Asian copper

grandfather died here, father died here, l will also die here

you are the only burial grounds

Asian copper, Asian copper

birds in love with doubt and flight, seawater submerges everything

your host is the green grass growing on your trim waist,

        guarding secrets and the palms of wildflowers

Asian copper, Asian copper

did you see? those two doves, they are Qu Yuan's * white shoes

        left behind on the beach

let us — together with the river, wear them

Asian copper, Asian copper

beat the drums, then call the hearts that dance in the

        darkness moon

this moon composed mainly of you

1984.10

---

* According to tradition, Qu Yuan (c. 340-278 BCE) is one of China's early great poets and
cultural figures. A loyal minister in the state of Chu, it is said that he gave wise counsel
to his king but was exiled because of jealous warring factions in the court. Upon hearing
the news that Chu had been defeated, Qu Yuan committed suicide by jumping into a river.
People living beside the river went out in boats in an effort to save him.

亚洲铜

亚洲铜，亚洲铜
祖父死在这里，父亲死在这里，我也将死在这里
你是唯一的一块埋人的地方

亚洲铜，亚洲铜
爱怀疑和爱飞翔的是鸟，淹没一切的是海水
你的主人却是青草，住在自己细小的腰上，
守住野花的手掌和秘密

亚洲铜，亚洲铜
看见了吗？那两只白鸽子，它是屈原遗落在沙滩上的白鞋子
让我们——我们和河流一起，穿上它吧

亚洲铜，亚洲铜
击鼓之后，我们把在黑暗中跳舞的心脏叫做月亮
这月亮主要由你构成

1984.10

THE HOUSE

In the morning
the first drop of dew you bump
is surely related to your lover
at noon watering your horse
beneath a young forking branch, this small moment
is also related to her
at dusk
you sit in your room, unmoving
this, too, is related to her

you can't deny it

massive sun concealed, sand and mud merging, fierce wind driving
the world raining, crying with affection
and this house of love tenderly sits
covering mother and covering son

covering you and covering me

1985

房屋

你在早上
碰落的第一滴露水
肯定和你的爱人有关
你在中午饮马
在一枝青丫下稍立片刻
也和她有关
你在暮色中
坐在屋子里，不动
还是与她有关

你不要不承认

巨日消隐，泥沙相合，狂风奔走
那雨天雨地哭得有情有意
而爱情房屋温情地坐着遮蔽母亲也遮蔽儿子

遮蔽你也遮蔽我

1985

WEDDING ON THE OCEAN

The bay's

blue hands

full of sleeping shipwrecks and islands

pairs of masts

falling in love in the wind

or parting

the wind blows into your

hair

a small brown net

thrown over my cheeks

in this life I will never cast it away

or like in the legends

we are the first

two people

living beyond the cliffs of some distant Arabian mountains

in an apple orchard

a snake and sunlight simultaneously slip into a small, beautiful river

you come

a green moon

dropping into the young cabin of my ship

海上婚礼

海湾
蓝色的手掌
睡满了沉船和岛屿
一对对桅杆
在风上相爱
或者分开

风吹起你的
头发
一张棕色的小网
撒满我的面颊
我一生也不想挣脱

或者如传说那样
我们就是最早的
两个人
住在遥远的阿拉伯山崖后面
苹果园里
蛇和阳光同时落入美丽的小河
你来了
一只绿色的月亮
掉进我年轻的船舱

LONGING FOR A PAST LIFE

Zhuangzi* washes his hands in the river
and after washing, there is silence on his palms
Zhuangzi washes himself
his body a bolt of cloth
thoroughly soaked
by the voices drifting over the river

Zhuangzi wants to work his way into
the wild beasts staring at the moon
bones inch by inch
above and below the navel
grow like tree branches

perhaps Zhuangzi is me
blindly feeling the bark of a tree
beginning intimacy with
my body
intimacy and also worries
moonlight touches me

it seems I am naked now
a naked body
entering, exiting

mother like a gate, softly opening to me

* Zhuangzi, who traditionally is said to have lived around the 4th century BCE,
is well-known in China as the putative author of one of China's most important
Daoist texts, which is also a work of high literary and philosophical value.

思念前生

庄子在水中洗手
洗完了手，手掌上一片寂静
庄子在水中洗身
身子是一匹布
那布上沾满了
水面上漂来漂去的声音

庄子想混入
凝望月亮的野兽
骨头一寸一寸
在肚脐上下
像树枝一样长着

也许庄子是我
摸一摸树皮
开始对自己的身子
亲切
亲切又苦恼
月亮触到我

仿佛我是光着身子
光着身子
进出

母亲如门，对我轻轻开着

LIVING ON THIS PRECIOUS EARTH

Living on this precious earth
sunlight is intense
water waves tender
layers of white clouds cover
me
treading through fresh green grass
I feel I am a thoroughly clean clump of dark soil

living on this precious earth
mud splashes high
splattering my cheeks
living on this precious earth
people as content as plants
love as content as rain

1985.1.12

活在珍贵的人间

活在这珍贵的人间
太阳强烈
水波温柔
一层层白云覆盖着
我
踩在青草上
感到自己是彻底干净的黑土块

活在这珍贵的人间
泥土高溅
扑打面颊
活在这珍贵的人间
人类和植物一样幸福
爱情和雨水一样幸福

1985.1.12

RIPE WHEAT

In that year
near Lanzhou, wheat
ripened anew

father
who drifted on the waters for more than thirty years
returned home

riding a sheep skin raft
returned home

someone shouldering wheat
in the night pushes open the door and enters

beneath the oil lamp
I now see clearly my third uncle

two brothers
one night without talk

only the water pipe
glug glug

our hearts are all
half-foot thick yellow earth
ripe wheat!

1985.1.20

熟了麦子

那一年
兰州一带的新麦
熟了

在水面上
混了三十多年的父亲
回家来

坐着羊皮筏子
回家来了

有人背着粮食
夜里推门进来

油灯下
认清是三叔

老哥俩
一宵无言

只有水烟锅
咕噜咕噜

谁的心思也是
半尺厚的黄土
熟了麦子呀！

1985.1.20

AT THE GATE OF THE NORTH

At the gate of the North
a small woman
rings a bell

I am willing
willing to be like a pagoda
erected silently in the night

as day breaks, she suddenly discovers me
looks up into the distance
and sees my full body beautiful

1985.2

北方门前

北方门前
一个小女人
在摇铃

我愿意
愿意像一座宝塔
在夜里悄悄建成

晨光中她突然发现我
她眺起眼睛
她看得我浑身美丽

1985.2

YOUR HANDS

The North

pulls at your hands

hands

pluck off gloves

they are two small lamps

my shoulders

are two old houses

that hold so much

they've even held the night

your hands

on top of them

illuminate them

and so, in the morning after our parting

in the light of dawn

I carry a bowl of porridge with both hands

thinking of two lamps

in the north

separated from me by mountains and rivers

that I can only distantly stroke

1985.2

你的手

北方
拉着你的手
手
摘下手套
她们就是两盏小灯

我的肩膀
是两座旧房子
容纳了那么多
甚至容纳过夜晚
你的手
在他上面
把他们照亮

于是有个别后的早上
在晨光中
我端起一碗粥
想起隔山隔水的
北方
有两盏灯

只能远远地抚摸

1985.2

I REQUEST: RAIN

I request extinguishing
the gleam of cast iron, the gleam of lovers and sunlight
I request a rain
I request
to die in the night

I request that in the morning
you come upon
those who bury me

the dust of years is endless
autumn
I request:
a rainfall
to wash my bones clean

my eyes close
I request:
rain
rain is a lifetime of mistakes
rain is grief and joy, separation and union

1985.3

我请求：雨

我请求熄灭
生铁的光、爱人的光和阳光
我请求下雨
我请求
在夜里死去

我请求在早上
你碰见
埋我的人

岁月的尘埃无边
秋天
我请求：
下一场雨
洗清我的骨头

我的眼睛合上
我请求：
雨
雨是一生过错
雨是悲欢离合

1985.3

WRITTEN FOR THE BODHISATTVA ON MY NECK

Breathe, breathe

we are two small jars

filled by warm vapor

placed together by Bodhisattva

Bodhisattva is an Eastern woman

she is very willing

to help

she helps you only once per life

and this is enough

passing through her

and passing through me

two hands happen upon you, your

写给脖子上的菩萨

呼吸，呼吸
我们是装满热气的
两只小瓶
被菩萨放在一起

菩萨是一位很愿意
帮忙的
东方女人
一生只帮你一次

这也足够了
通过她
也通过我自己
双手碰到了你，你的

breath

two trembling little red sails
held between my lips
Bodhisattva knows
Bodhisattva lives in a bamboo forest
she knows everything
knows tonight
knows all compassion
knows seawater is me
washing your eyebrows
knows on my body you breathe, breathe

Bodhisattva's willing
Bodhisattva's heart is very willing
to let me be born
to let my mature body
be draped by a damp you

1985.4

呼吸

两片抖动的小红帆
含在我的唇间
菩萨知道
菩萨住在竹林里
她什么都知道
知道今晚
知道一切恩情
知道海水是我
洗着你的眉
知道你就在找我身上呼吸，呼吸

菩萨愿意
菩萨心里非常愿意
就让我出生
让我长成的身体上
挂着潮湿的你

1985.4

WHEAT FIELDS

Grown up on wheat
carrying big bowls under the moonlight
in the bowls, the moon
and wheat
without a sound

unlike you two
when singing the wheat field's praises
I must also sing of the moon

under the moon
my father sowing wheat throughout the night
his body flowing gold

under the moon
twelve birds
fly across the wheat lands
some plucking up grains
some dancing in the wind, defying it

麦地

吃麦子长大的
在月亮下端着大碗
碗内的月亮
和麦子
一直没有声响

和你俩不一样
在歌颂麦地时
我要歌颂月亮

月亮下
连夜种麦的父亲
身上像流动金子

月亮下
有十二只鸟
飞过麦田
有的衔起一颗麦粒
有的则迎风起舞，矢口否认

looking at the wheat, I sleep in the fields
the moon illuminates me like shining in a well
hometown's wind
hometown's clouds
gather their wings
and sleep on my shoulders

waves of wheat —
heaven's table
set in the open country
the wheat fields

in the reaping season
waves of wheat and moonlight
wash our sharp sickles

the moon knows I am
sometimes more weary than mud
my shy lover
swaying
wheat straw

we are the wheat field's beloved
today harvesting wheat, me and my enemies
grasp hands and speak peacefully
finish the work together

and close our eyes, in this moment we contentedly accept
each fated thing

看麦子时我睡在地里
月亮照我如照一口井
家乡的风
家乡的云
收聚翅膀
睡在我的双肩

麦浪——
天堂的桌子
摆在田野上
一块麦地

收割季节
麦浪和月光
洗着快镰刀

月亮知道我
有时比泥土还要累
而羞涩的情人
眼前晃动着
麦秸

我们是麦地的心上人
收麦这天我和仇人
握手言和

我们一起干完活
合上眼睛，命中注定的一切
此刻我们心满意足地接受

wives excitedly

wipe hands

on white aprons

as the moon illuminates the earth

each of us leads

the Nile, Babylon, or the Yellow River's

children on the banks of the rivers

on the islands where bees flutter or on the plains

to wash hands

and prepare to eat

then let me have you inside like this

let me speak like this

the moon is not burdened by sorrow

under the moon

there are only two people

the poor and the rich

New York and Jerusalem

and me

us three

dreaming together of wheat fields beyond the cities

white poplars surround

healthy wheat fields

healthy wheat

wheat that brings life!

1985.6

妻子们兴奋地
不停用白围裙
擦手

这时正当月光普照大地
我们各自领着
尼罗河、巴比伦或黄河
的孩子在河流两岸
在群蜂飞舞的岛屿或平原
洗了手
准备吃饭

就让我这样把你们包括进来吧
让我这样说
月亮并不忧伤
月亮下
一共有两个人
穷人和富人
纽约和耶路撒冷
还有我
我们三个人
一同梦到了城市外面的麦地
白杨树围住的
健康的麦地
健康的麦子
养我性命的麦子！

1985.6

FOURTEEN LINES: NIGHT MOON

Pushing open the forest

sun puts its blood

into our lanterns

I quietly sit

in the village

in the place where people live

everything is the same as its root self

everything is deposited

on the faces of generations

every misfortune

it seems I

am a well dug by ancestors

towards later generations.

every misfortune begins in my deep, calm, and mysterious waters

1985.6.19

十四行：夜晚的月亮

推开树林
太阳把血
放入灯盏

我静静坐在
人的村庄
人居住的地方
一切都和本原一样
一切都存入
人的世世代代的脸
一切不幸

我仿佛
一口祖先们
向后代挖掘的井
一切不幸都源于我幽深而神秘的水

1985.6.19

UNTITLED

Give me grain

give me a wedding

give me stars and horses

give me a song

give me the deepest rest!

my birthday

a beautiful

tormentor, a female captive

sitting on her hometown's wheat threshing floor

beneath the moonlight

entrancing the village idlers!

无题

给我粮食
给我婚礼
给我星辰和马匹
给我歌曲
给我安息!

我的生日
这是位美丽的
折磨人的女俘虏
坐在故乡的打麦场上

在月光下
使村子里的二流子
如痴如醉!

SPRING

You come head on
ice thaws and snow melts
you come head on
the earth faintly quivers

the earth faintly quivers
having endured it's suffering
on this festival day
why are you so sad

wildflowers are wine glasses at the night's wedding feast
wildflowers are the bride at the night's wedding feast
wildflowers are the colorful rooftop
with which I cover my bride

the snow bundled you far away
everything depends on the sound of the wind slipping by
o, spring
spring is my essence

春天

你迎面走来
冰消雪融
你迎面走来
大地微微颤栗

大地微微颤栗
曾经饱经忧患
在这个节日里
你为什么更加惆怅

野花是一夜喜筵的酒杯
野花是一夜喜筵的新娘
野花是我包容新娘
的彩色屋顶

白雪抱你远去
全凭风声默默流逝
春天啊
春天是我的品质

SOLITUDE IN CHANGPING

Solitude is a fish basket
is spring water in a fish basket
put in spring water

solitude is the deer king sleeping in spring water
the deer hunter he dreamt of
the one carrying water with a fish basket

along with the other solitudes
it's two sons in a cypress boat
and every daughter, revolving around the Book of Songs, mulberry and
     hemp, the Yuan and Xiang Rivers, wood and leaves*
defeated in love
they are a flame in the fish basket
sinking to the water's bottom

pulled to shore it is still a fish basket
solitude can't be said

1986

* Hai Zi makes several references to classical Chinese literature in these lines. The Book of
Songs is a well-known book of early Chinese poetry, with poems dating perhaps as far back
as the late second millennium BCE. It includes two poems titled 柏舟 (Cypress Boat), both
of which recount scenes of loneliness and pain at separation. The Yuan and Xiang Rivers
probably refer to the classical poem, "Sorrow after Departure" (离骚), which recounts the
virtuous author's life and his lonely travels to the south after various political and personal
rejections. The relevant line reads "Crossing the Yuan and Xiang Rivers I journeyed
south"(济沅湘以南征兮).

在昌平的孤独

孤独是一只鱼筐
是鱼筐中的泉水
放在泉水中

孤独是泉水中睡着的鹿王
梦见的猎鹿人
就是那用鱼筐提水的人

以及其他的孤独
是柏木之舟中的两个儿子
和所有女儿，围着诗经桑麻沅湘木叶
在爱情中失败
他们是鱼筐中的火苗
沉到水底

拉到岸上还是一只鱼筐
孤独不可言说

1986

BODIES (II)

Bodies are beautiful
bodies are the forest's
only living body
bodies are beautiful

bodies, firmly distant from other treasures
firmly distant from other mysterious brothers

bodies stand alone
seeing birds and fish

bodies sleep on the banks of rivers
brides of rain and forests
sleeping on the banks of rivers

over the earth hung with millet
the body of the sun
rises and falls, illuminating all
like silent
treasures and villages
on a festival day

only bodies are beautiful

肉体（之二）

肉体美丽
肉体是树林中
唯一活着的肉体
肉体美丽

肉体，远离其他的财宝
远离其他的神秘兄弟

肉体独自站立
看见了鸟和鱼

肉体睡在河水两岸
雨和森林的新娘
睡在河水两岸

垂着谷子的大地上
太阳的肉体
一升一落，照耀四方
像寂静的
节日的
财宝和村庄

只有肉体美丽

WILDFLOWERS, BRIGHT DAUGHTERS OF THE SUN

Wives of sorrow and rivers
grateful for approaching bodies
grateful for the attachment of souls
(bodies are the lyre of wildflowers
covering the skeleton's wine glass)

grateful for my own heavy skeleton
that can also dream

bodies are dreams of the river
bodies see people picking fennel and approaching spring water

bodies are beautiful
bodies are the forest's
only living body
dying in the forest

approaching graveyards
bodies are beautiful

1986

野花，太阳明亮的女儿

河川和忧愁的妻子
感激肉体来临　感激灵魂有所附丽
（肉体是野花的琴
盖住骨骼的酒杯）

感激我自己沉重的骨骼
也能做梦

肉体是河流的梦
肉体看见了采茴香的人迎着泉水

肉体美丽
肉体是树林中
唯一活着的肉体
死在树林里

迎着墓地
肉体美丽

1986

POEM ON DEATH (I)

In pitch-black night a laughter that snaps the planks of my tomb
you know: this is the tiger burial grounds

as a fire-red tiger crosses the water
your laughter
breaks two bones of
the tiger floating in the river
as the river freezes in the black laughter night
the broken-legged tiger floats down river to my
window

the planks of the tiger's burial pit
snapped in two by laughter

死亡之诗（之一）

漆黑的夜里有一种笑声笑断我坟墓的木板
你可知道，这是一片埋葬老虎的土地

正当水面上渡过一只火红的老虎
你的笑声使河流漂浮
的老虎
断了两根骨头
正在这条河流开始在存有笑声的黑夜里结冰
断腿的老虎顺河而下，来到我的
窗前

一块埋葬老虎的木板
被一种笑声笑断两截

POEM ON DEATH (II: PICKING SUNFLOWERS)
— A SMALL NARRATIVE FOR VAN GOGH: THE PROCESS OF SUICIDE

On a rainy night a cow thief

climbs in my window

and on my dreaming body

picks sunflowers

I remain deeply asleep

and on my dreaming body

colorful sunflowers bloom

those picking hands

still seem like beautiful and clumsy doves

in a field of sunflowers

死亡之诗（之二：采摘葵花）
——给凡·高的小叙事：自杀过程

雨夜偷牛的人
爬进了我的窗户
在我做梦的身子上
采摘葵花

我仍在沉睡
在我睡梦的身子上
开放了彩色的葵花
那双采摘的
仍像葵花田
美丽笨拙的鸽子

on a rainy night a cow thief

steals me

from my temporal body

I am still deeply sleeping

I am taken beyond my body

beyond the sunflowers, I am the world's

first cow (the empress of death)

I feel that I am beautiful

I am still deeply sleeping

on a rainy night the cow thief

because of this is rapturous

he becomes another colorful cow

running with mad glee

in my body

雨夜偷牛的人
把我从人类
身体中偷走
我仍在沉睡
我被带到身体之外
葵花之外，我是世界上
第一头母牛（死的皇后）
我觉得自己很美
我仍在沉睡

雨夜偷牛的人
于是非常高兴
自己变成了另外的彩色母牛
在我的身体中
兴高采烈地奔跑

NATURE

Let me tell you
she is a beautiful and robust woman
little blue fish are her water pots
and the clothing she slips off
she loves you with her flesh
in folk songs she's loved you for a very long time

you're looking everywhere
sometimes you fumble into her body
you sit atop logs kissing her
every leaf her lips
but you are blind to her
you have always been blind to her

she still loves you from a distant place

大自然

让我来告诉你
她是一位美丽结实的女子
蓝色小鱼是她的水罐
也是她脱下的服装
她会用肉体爱你
在民歌中久久地爱你

你上上下下瞧着
你有时摸到了她的身子
你坐在圆木头上亲她
每一片木叶都是她的嘴唇
但你看不见她
你仍然看不见她

她仍在远处爱着你

IN *REQUIEM* MOZART SAYS

The women that I can see
women in the water
in the wheat fields please
sort through my bones
like reed catkins
pack them into the body of my violin and carry them back

the women that I can see
pure women, women
of the river
please reach out your hands to the wheat fields

when I am hopeless
sitting on a bundle of wheat returning home
please put my bones, once scattered, in order
put them in that little dark red chest, carry them back
like carrying back your lavish dowry

莫扎特在《安魂曲》中说

我所能看见的妇女
水中的妇女
请在麦地之中
清理好我的骨头
如一束芦花的骨头
把它装在琴箱里带回

我所能看见的
洁净的妇女，河流
上的妇女
请把手伸到麦地之中

当我没有希望
坐在一束麦子上回家
请整理好我那零乱的骨头
放入那暗红色的小木柜，带回它
像带回你们富裕的嫁妆

THE SWAN

In the night, the sounds of swans flying across a distant bridge
the river in my body
responds to them

as they fly across the mud of birthing days, the mud of dusk
there is a wounded swan
only the beautiful, whipping wind knows
she is wounded. and she keeps flying

the river inside my body is so heavy
heavy like a door hanging on a house
as they fly across the distant bridge
I cannot respond to them with my own exquisite flight

they fly like heavy snow over a graveyard
in the heavy snow there is no through path to my door
— bodies have no doors — only fingers
stuck in a graveyard, like ten frostbitten candles

in my mud
in the mud of birthing days
there is a wounded swan
just like the folk singer sings

天鹅

夜里，我听见远处天鹅飞越桥梁的声音
我身体里的河水
呼应着她们

当她们飞越生日的泥土、黄昏的泥土
有一只天鹅受伤
其实只有美丽吹动的风才知道
她已受伤。她仍在飞行

而我身体里的河水却很沉重
就像房屋上挂着的门扇一样沉重
当她们飞过一座远方的桥梁
我不能用优美的飞行来呼应她们

当她们像大雪飞过墓地
大雪中却没有路通向我的房门
——身体没有门——只有手指
竖在墓地，如同十根冻伤的蜡烛

在我的泥土上
在生日的泥土上
有一只天鹅受伤
正如民歌手所唱

TEARS

On the last peak leaves slowly redden
mountains like a poor child's gray and white horses
on this last night of October
dipped in a pool of blood

on this last night of October
a poor child carries a lantern though the night returning home
    tears on his face
and everything dies halfway in some small village far from its
    native place
on this last night of October

someone leaning against the white tavern wall
asks after the people buried in the bean fields of his hometown
on this last night of October
asks who do the white horses and gray horses die for... fresh
blood deep red

do their masters return home carrying their lanterns
do the spirits of autumn go with them
are they all ghosts
running mad down the paths of the under world

do the spirits open the window for me
tossing out this tattered old poetry collection for me
on this last night of October
I will not write of you again

泪水

最后的山顶树叶渐红
群山似穷孩子的灰马和白马
在十月的最后一夜
倒在血泊中

在十月的最后一夜
穷孩子夜里提灯还家泪流满面
一切死于中途　在远离故乡的小镇上
在十月的最后一夜

背靠酒馆白墙的那个人
问起家乡的豆子地里埋葬的人
在十月的最后一夜
问起白马和灰马为谁而死……鲜血殷红

他们的主人是否提灯还家
秋天之魂是否陪伴着他
他们是否都是死人
都在阴间的道路上疯狂奔驰

是否此魂替我打开窗户
替我扔出一本破旧的诗集
在十月的最后一夜
我从此不再写你

FOR MOTHER

1. Wind

Wind is beautiful, fruits are beautiful
a gentle breeze is beautiful
the breasts of nature are also beautiful

water is beautiful   o, water
the moment
when no one is speaking to you is beautiful

your home's shabby door
hiding your poverty is beautiful

wind blows over the grasslands
and horse bones turn green

给母亲

1. 风

风很美果实也美
小小的风很美
自然界的乳房也美

水很美水啊
无人和你
说话的时刻很美

你家中破旧的门
遮住的贫穷很美

风　吹遍草原
马的骨头　绿了

2. Spring Water

Spring   spring
the lips of life
a blue mother
using her body
using a zither of wildflowers
to cover the rocks
to cover bones and wine glasses

2. 泉水

泉水　泉水
生物的嘴唇
蓝色的母亲
用肉体
用野花的琴
盖住岩石
盖住骨头和酒杯

3. Clouds

Mother

you are old now, white hair hanging down

mother, you should rest

your quiet sons lie on the hillside

like quiet water on the slopes

flowing into the sky

I sing the praises of the clouds

sisters of rain

a beautiful proposal of marriage

I know there is no use for my love poems with which I serenade

    my lover

I sing the praises of the clouds

I know that finally I will be happy

with every holy and pure person

together in heaven

3. 云

母亲
老了，垂下白发
母亲你去休息吧
山坡上伏着安静的儿子
就像山腰安静的水
流着天空

我歌唱云朵
雨水的姐妹
美丽的求婚
我知道自己颂扬情侣的诗歌没有了用场

我歌唱云朵
我知道自己终究会幸福
和一切圣洁的人
相聚在天堂

4. Snow

Mother sits again on the small stool in our hometown, thinking
    of me
that stool like my rooftop collecting snow

mother's rooftop
tomorrow morning's
sun-streaked sky

I want to see you
mother, mother
you face the granary
stepping into dusk
you age with each passing day

4. 雪

妈妈又坐在家乡的矮凳子上想我
那一只凳子仿佛是我积雪的屋顶

妈妈的屋顶
明天早上
霞光万道

我要看到你
妈妈，妈妈
你面朝谷仓
脚踏黄昏
我知道你日见衰老

5. Language and a Well

Language in itself
is like a mother
always something to say, at the riverside
on the banks of the river of experience
on the banks of the river of phenomena
flowers like a gentle wife
carefully listening ears and poems
growing all over
carefully listen to the suffering of the water

water flows to a distant place

1984

1985 revised

1986 revised again

5. 语言和井

语言的本身
像母亲
总有话说，在河畔
在经验之河的两岸
在现象之河的两岸
花朵像柔美的妻子
倾听的耳朵和诗歌
长满一地
倾听受难的水

水落在远方

1984
1985 改
1986 再改

DUNHUANG*

Dunhuang caves like wooden casks
hanging beneath horse's bellies
the ear splitting sound of milk dripping—
like someone on the distant grasslands ripping at their ears
coming to this last valley
with flowers hanging
from his torn-up ears

Dunhuang is a forest
where there was a great fire a thousand years ago
in an unknown valley
it's the last mulberry forest - I traded
salt and grain here
I dug these grottoes, before death I painted you
an image of the last handsome male
for a mother squirrel
for a queen bee
to allow them to once again conceive in spring

1986

* Dunhuang is a place in western China where in 1900 a large hoard of
early manuscripts and art dating mostly from about 400 -1,000 AD., many
of them religious in nature, were discovered in man-made caves. The
discovery has been invaluable for understanding early Chinese culture.
Hai Zi visited the site in 1986.

敦煌

敦煌石窟像马肚子下
挂着一只只木桶
乳汁的声音滴破耳朵——
像远方草原上撕破耳朵的人
来到这最后的山谷
他撕破的耳朵上
悬挂着花朵

敦煌是千年以前
起了大火的森林
在陌生的山谷
是最后的桑林——我交换
食盐和粮食的地方
我筑下岩洞，在死亡之前，画上你
最后一个美男子的形象
为了一只母松鼠
为了一只母蜜蜂
为了让她们在春天再次怀孕

1986

JULY IS NOT FAR
— FOR QINGHAI LAKE*, PLEASE EXTINGUISH MY LOVE

July is not far

the birth of the sexes is not far

love is not far—under the horse's nose

salt in the lake

so, the Qinghai cannot be far

at the lakeside, beehives

make me so dismal and enchanting:

green grass bloomed with wildflowers

at Qinghai Lake

my solitude is like the horses of heaven

(and so, the horses of heaven are not far)

I am the Romantic: poems chanting of wildflowers

the only poisonous wildflower in the bellies of heaven's horses

(Qinghai Lake, please extinguish my love!)

七月不远
——给青海湖，请熄灭我的爱情

七月不远
性别的诞生不远
爱情不远——马鼻子下
湖泊含盐

因此青海不远
湖畔一捆捆蜂箱
使我显得凄凄迷人：
青草开满鲜花

青海湖上
我的孤独如天堂的马匹
（因此，天堂的马匹不远）

我就是那个情种：诗中吟唱的野花
天堂的马肚子里唯一含毒的野花
（青海湖，请熄灭我的爱情！）

the new sprouts of wildflowers are not far, the ancient family

names in the medicine chest are not far

(other drifters, their sicknesses cured

have returned home, I want to join you)

and so, this arduous journey of death is not far

my skeleton hung with my body

like tree branches on blue water

o Qinghai Lake, your water in boundless dusk

everything is as it is right now!

only the vitality of May, flocks of birds who flew away long ago

the first bird who drank down my precious jewels flew away

    long ago

only Qinghai Lake remains, this jeweled corpse

       water in boundless dusk

1986

*Qinghai Lake is a large saline body of water which is on a variety of bird
migration routes. Hai Zi visited Qinghai Lake in 1980 during his travels to
western China.

野花青梗不远，医箱内古老姓氏不远
（其他的浪子，治好了疾病
已回原籍，我这就想去见你们）

因此跋山涉水死亡不远
骨骼挂遍我身体
如同蓝色水上的树枝

啊，青海湖，暮色苍茫的水面
一切如在眼前！

只有五月生命的鸟群早已飞去
只有饮我宝石的头一只鸟早已飞去
只剩下青海湖，这宝石的尸体
　　　　　暮色苍茫的水面

1986

VILLAGE

Village, in this rich harvest village, I settle in
the fewer things I happen to touch the better!
this village that treasures dusk, this village that treasures rain
10,000 cloudless miles mirror my eternal sorrow

1986

村庄

村庄，在五谷丰盛的村庄，我安顿下来
我顺手摸到的东西越少越好！
珍惜黄昏的村庄，珍惜雨水的村庄
万里无云如同我永恒的悲伤

1986

SEVEN STARS OF THE BIG DIPPER, SEVEN VILLAGES
— FOR THE GIRL OF EJINA WHO I MET BY CHANCE

Village   roof beams floated here on the water drifting
ten more days   and I will end this drifting life
and return to a village of abundant harvest   village of the
    abandoned orchards
the village   where you live deep in the desert   Ejina!

autumn's winds come early here   autumn's winds whip
silently facing Ejina
beneath white poplars I blow out your eyes
Ejina   silently sleeping in this great desert

Ejina girl   my dark and graceful girl
your lips are telling and singing
the winds of the harvest blow across camels, cows, and sheep
churning the desert   you are the unforgettable girl of this town

1986

北斗七星　七座村庄
——献给萍水相逢的额济纳姑娘

村庄　水上运来的房梁　漂泊不定
还有十天　我就要结束　漂泊的生涯
回到五谷丰盛的村庄　废弃果园的村庄
村庄是沙漠深处你所居住的地方　额济纳！

秋天的风早早地吹　秋天的风　高高地吹
静静面对额济纳
白杨树下我吹灭你的两只眼睛
额济纳　大沙漠上静静地睡

额济纳姑娘　我黑而秀美的姑娘
你的嘴唇在诉说　在歌唱
五谷的风儿吹过骆驼和牛羊
翻过沙漠　你是镇子上最令人难忘的姑娘

1986

SEPTEMBER CLOUDS

September clouds
unfolding burial cloths

September clouds
bright and clear clouds

compelled to do so on a plate, I
carve poetry and clouds

I love these beautiful clouds

gleaming on the water
river pushing forward

my words surging like a stream
loving these beautiful clouds

1986

九月的云

九月的云
展开殓布

九月的云
晴朗的云

被迫在盘子上，我
刻下诗句和云

我爱这美丽的云

水上有光
河水向前

我一向言语滔滔
我爱着美丽的云

1986

SEPTEMBER

Witness the wildflowers on the grasslands where gods come to die

the wind – more distant than the furthest places

my zither cries out   with no more tears

I return the distance of distant places to the grasslands

one is called the head of my horse one the tail*

my zither cries out with no more tears

in the distance there are only wildflowers gathered in death

the bright moon like a mirror hung high above the grasslands, shines

    down on a thousand years

my zither cries out   with no more tears

alone whipping my horse across the grasslands

1986

*This apparently refers to the horse-headed qin (here translated as zither), a traditional musical instrument used by horse-riding Mongolian people. The instrument is so named because its body is traditionally made from horses' head. The strings and bow of the instrument are made from horse hair.

九月

目击众神死亡的草原上野花一片
远在远方的风比远方更远
我的琴声呜咽　泪水全无
我把这远方的远归还草原
一个叫马头　一个叫马尾
我的琴声呜咽　泪水全无

远方只有在死亡中凝聚野花一片
明月如镜高悬草原映照千年岁月
我的琴声呜咽　泪水全无
只身打马过草原

1986

AUTUMN RECALLS THE SUFFERING
OF SPRING AND RECALLS LEI FENG*

Spring   spring

so transient

spring's life of suffering

a life of contentment

thinking again of you crashing through the door cradling the spring

you sit down. sit down now, in this crazy place

spring's life of suffering

a life of contentment

spring   spring   spring's life of suffering

my village has a noble man named Uncle Lei Feng

spring's life of suffering

a life of contentment

these days I've grown bigger even than Lei Feng

in the village the suffering goddesses peacefully fall to sleep

spring's life of suffering

a life of contentment

1985
1987

* Starting in the 1960s, propaganda posters, books, and slogans featured Lei Feng as
their larger-than-life subject. He was a Chinese peasant who became a model worker
and joined the People's Liberation Army. According to official accounts he performed
many selfless deeds for the good of the people and the Communist Party. Chinese
art and literature of that time period was based on clear, simple symbolism and often
repetitious political messages which unambiguously supported the Party, Socialism
and the proletariat class. Today, Lei Feng is a highly recognizable figure in China.

秋日想起春天的痛苦 也想起雷锋

春天　春天
他何其短暂
春天的一生痛苦
他一生幸福

又想起你撞开门扇你怀抱春天
你坐下。快坐下，在这如痴如醉的地方
春天的一生痛苦
他一生幸福

春天　春天　春天的一生痛苦
我的村庄中有一个好人叫雷锋叔叔
春天的一生痛苦
他一生幸福

如今我长得比雷锋还大
村庄中痛苦女神安然入睡
春天的一生痛苦
他一生幸福

1985
1987

HIMALAYA

Plateau hanging in the sky

sky rolls toward me

I lose everything

before me a great sea

I am in my own distant place

on the seabed of my native place -

I walk in the altitudes of earth's highest place

Himalaya   Himalaya

who are you

starving

pregnant

put the endless

skulls that have rolled across the sky

back in the sky

from the great sea I come to the center of the setting sun

flying all over the sky I find no place to alight

now there is grain, but no hunger

喜马拉雅

高原悬在天空
天空向我滚来
我丢失了一切
面前只有大海

我是在我自己的远方
我在故乡的海底——
走过世界最高的地方
喜马拉雅　喜马拉雅

你是谁
饥饿
怀孕
把无尽的
滚过天空的头颅
放回天空

我从大海来到落日的中央
飞遍了天空找不到一块落脚之地
今日有粮食却没有饥饿

today grain flies across the sky
unable to find an empty belly
grain feeds hunger
even greater hunger, on the verge of death
the sky of the grasslands is irresistible

lips and me embrace river water
a skull and his sisters
in the bottom of the great river flowing toward the sea
bodies with their severed skulls remain in the world
the highest mountain
still growing up

今天的粮食飞遍了天空
找不到一只饥饿的腹部
饥饿用粮食喂养
更加饥饿，奄奄一息
草原上的天空不可阻挡

嘴唇和我抱住河水
头颅和他的姐妹
在大河底部通向海洋
割下头颅的身子仍在世上
最高的一座山
仍在向上生长

VILLAGE OF NINE POEMS

The beauty of an autumn night
makes my former affections difficult to forget
I sit on the faintly warmed earth
accompanied by grain and water
nine old poems from the past
like nine beautiful villages in autumn
making my former affections difficult to forget

when being ploughed and sown, the earth
says nothing, it lives in its native place
like water drops, a rich harvest, or defeat
live in my heart

1987

九首诗的村庄

秋夜美丽
使我旧情难忘
我坐在微温的地上
陪伴粮食和水
九首过去的旧诗
像九座美丽的秋天下的村庄
使我旧情难忘

大地在耕种
一语不发，住在家乡像水滴、丰收或失败
住在我心上

1987

TWO VILLAGES

A village of peace and a village of sexual desire

villages of poetry

the village mother flowers only briefly

her beauty unsurpassed

on May wheat fields villages of the swans

reticent, lonely villages

one in front, one behind

my and Pushkin's birth places

wind blows through the villages

wind blows through Hai Zi's villages

wind blows through the winds of the villages

one gust fresh and new, one old and musty

两座村庄

和平与情欲的村庄
诗的村庄
村庄母亲昙花一现
村庄母亲美丽绝伦

五月的麦地上   天鹅的村庄
沉默孤独的村庄
一个在前一个在后
这就是普希金和我   诞生的地方

风吹在村庄
风吹在海子的村庄
风吹在村庄的风上
有一阵新鲜有一阵久远

northern starlight shines on the constellations of the south
at the village mother's bosom Pushkin and me
poets of girls and schools of fish sleeping peacefully in raindrops
it is the rain drops that will die!

in the night the wind whips listen as it blows through the villages
the villages silently sit like pitch-dark treasures
two villages sleep, separated by a river
Hai Zi's village sleeps deeper still

1987.2 draft
1987.5 revised

北方星光照映南国星座
村庄母亲怀中的普希金和我
闺女和鱼群的诗人　女睡在雨滴中
是雨滴就会死亡！

夜里风大　听风吹在村庄
村庄静坐像黑漆漆的财宝
两座村庄隔河而睡
海子的村庄睡得更沉

1987.2 草稿
1987.5 改

Question

Running through young wheat fields
snow and sun radiance

poet, you are powerless to repay
the true friendship of wheat fields and radiance

a type of desire
a type of kindness
you are powerless to repay

you are powerless to repay
a star emitting radiance
above your head combusting in loneliness

麦地与诗人

询问

在青麦地上跑着
雪和太阳的光芒

诗人，你无力偿还
麦地和光芒的情义

一种愿望
一种善良
你无力偿还

你无力偿还
一颗放射光芒的星辰
在你头顶寂寞燃烧

Answer

Wheat fields
others see you
and think you warm and beautiful
but I stand at the center of your painful interrogation
             scorched by you
I stand in the sun   painful awns of wheat

wheat fields
mysterious interrogators

I stand painfully before you
you cannot say I have nothing
you cannot say I am empty-handed

wheat fields, humanity's pain
is the poetry and radiance we emit!

1987

答复

麦地
别人看见你
觉得你温暖，美丽
我则站在你痛苦质问的中心
                被你灼伤
我站在太阳　痛苦的芒上

麦地
神秘的质问者啊

当我痛苦地站在你的面前
你不能说我一无所有
你不能说我两手空空

麦地啊，人类的痛苦
是他放射的诗歌和光芒！

1987

REBUILDING THE HOMELAND

Out on the river abandon wisdom
don't look to the vast sky
for your existence you must cry tears of humiliation
that irrigate the homeland

existence requires no insight
the earth reveals itself
with our contentment and our suffering
rebuilds the rooftops of our hometowns

abandon contemplation and wisdom
and if you cannot bring grains of wheat
then for this honest earth please
maintain silence   and your dark nature

wind blows the smoke from kitchen chimneys
the nearby orchard quietly howls
"labor with both hands
    and so console your spirit"

1987

重建家园

在水上　放弃智慧
停止仰望长空
为了生存你要流下屈辱的泪水
来浇灌家园

生存无须洞察
大地自己呈现
用幸福也用痛苦
来重建家乡的屋顶

放弃沉思和智慧
如果不能带来麦粒
请对诚实的大地
保持缄默　和你那幽暗的本性

风吹炊烟
果园就在我的身旁静静叫喊
　"双手劳动
　　慰藉心灵"

1987

MOONLIGHT

Tonight's beautiful moonlight   look how enchanting it is!
illuminating moonlight
a horse drinking water and salt
and voices

tonight's beautiful moonlight   look how amazing it is
in the sheep herd the quiet voices of life and death
l am listening carefully!

a ballad of earth and water, moonlight!

do not say that you are the light in the light   moonlight!

do not say there is a place in your heart
a place I do not dare dream of
do not ask   about the way peaches are the hidden treasures of
      peach blossoms
do not ask   about the wheat threshing earth virgins
          osmanthus flowers and villages
tonight's beautiful moonlight   look how enchanting it is!

月光

今夜美丽的月光　你看多好!
照着月光
饮水和盐的马
和声音

今夜美丽的月光　你看多美丽
羊群中　生命和死亡宁静的声音
我在倾听!

这是一支大地和水的歌谣，月光!

不要说　你是灯中之灯　月光!

不要说心中有一个地方
那是我一直不敢梦见的地方
不要问　桃子对桃花的珍藏
不要问　打麦大地　处女　桂花和村镇
今夜美丽的月光　你看多好!

do not say that the death candle has been uselessly toppled
living things still grow everywhere on this sad river
moonlight illuminating moonlight   illuminating all things
tonight, flows of beautiful moonlight converge

1986.7 draft

1987.5 revised

不要说死亡的烛光何须倾倒
生命依然生长在忧愁的河水上
月光照着月光   月光普照
今夜美丽的月光合在一起流淌

1986.7 初稿
1987.5 改

IN MY NATIVE PLACE

Birds   in my native place like blue hands or wombs
hands and wombs
from the deathly silence of stones, you ascend without a thought

sheep herds...many hooves coming and going   dying over and over
the earth shines...horses of the moon fly to snow mountains
                and villages
women chose names for growing broad bean flowers, "moon"

"recall our bulging breasts
we want to smash the cabin of this ship
does the solitary captain often think of us..."

the dark queen is my precious sword of immortal youth
the lion dances below the church
you should join him! although I have no voice! you should
                answer! you should make a noise!

在家乡

鸟　在家乡如一只蓝色的手或者子宫
手和子宫
你从石头死寂中茫然无知地上升

羊群……许多蹄子来了又去　反复灭绝
大地发光……月亮的马　飞到雪山和村庄
女人取了一个生蚕豆花的名字"月亮"

"回想我们高高隆起的乳房
总想砸烂船舱
那船长是否独自一人常把我们回想……"

阴暗的女王就是我永远青春的宝剑
当狮子在教堂下舞蹈
你应呼应！即使我没有声音！你应回答！你应发出声音！

a water jug sways walking high into the mountain peaks growing into
    caves and homes
a great bird eating a stalk of wheat
ancestors who spent their lives in labor

skulls, lonely stars, suffering stars, bright stars, my heart, sitting on a
    skull screaming
I open the first dragon bone, the second bone, I will in the third cold-
    resistant season crawl
crawl into its body, I must avoid my own pursuit/attack

in the dangerous open county
where corpses are laid down
that is our native place

on the mountaintop my free corpse covers me emitting the shy fragrance
    of flowers

1987 (?)

水罐摇摇晃晃走上山巅成长为洞窟和房屋
大鸟食麦一株
祖先们更在劳动中丧生

头盖骨，孤独的星，忧伤的星，明亮的星，我的心，坐在头颅上
　　大叫大嚷
我打开龙的第一只骨头，第二只骨头，我将会在第三个耐寒的
　　季节里爬
爬进它的身体，我将躲我自己的追击

在危险的原野上
落下尸体的地方
那就是家乡

我的自由的尸体在山上将我遮盖　放出花朵的
羞涩香味

1987（？）

MAY WHEAT FIELDS

All brothers of the world
embrace in the wheat fields
East, South, North and West
four brothers of the wheat fields, good brothers
recalling the past
each reciting their own poem
embracing in wheat fields

sometimes I sit alone
in May wheat fields   dreaming in vain of all my brothers
see the pebbles in my native place rolled to the riversides
at dusk the eternally arced sky
covering the villages of the earth with sorrow
sometimes I sit alone in wheat fields, reciting Chinese poems
      for my brothers
without eyes and without lips

1987.5

五月的麦地

全世界的兄弟们
要在麦地里拥抱
东方，南方，北方和西方
麦地里的四兄弟，好兄弟
回顾往昔
背诵各自的诗歌
要在麦地里拥抱

有时我孤独一人坐下
在五月的麦地　梦想众兄弟
看到家乡的卵石滚满了河滩
黄昏常存弧形的天空
让大地上布满哀伤的村庄
有时我孤独一人坐在麦地为众兄弟
背诵中国诗歌
没有了眼睛也没有了嘴唇

1987.5

THE NORTH WOODS

Locust trees bloom at the foot of the mountains
we have walked this path together
to lie on mountain slopes   experiencing boundless dusk
distant mountains like visions   silently lingering

picking locust blossoms
locust blossoms emitting fragrance in my hand
fragrance   from the earth's endless sorrow
the earth has been alone   and will be alone

this is dusk at the end of spring in the north
white poplars whistle   verdant vegetation
faint red clouds at last motionless
see the pine trees swollen with balsam

yes, on the mountaintops there are only locust, poplar, and pine
we sit   experiencing boundless dusk
could this be our dusk
a faint wind blows from the wheat fields   in a moment sinking
    into darkness

1987.5

北方的树林

槐树在山脚开花
我们一路走来
躺在山坡上　感受茫茫黄昏
远山像幻觉　默默停留一会

摘下槐花
槐花在手中放出香味
香味　来自大地无尽的忧伤
大地孑然一身　至今仍孑然一身

这是一个北方暮春的黄昏
白杨萧萧　草木葱茏
淡红色云朵在最后静止不动
看见了饱含香脂的松树

是啊，山上只有槐树　杨树和松树
我们坐下　感受茫茫黄昏
莫非这就是你我的黄昏
麦田吹来微风　顷刻沉入黑暗

1987.5

THE DAY OF CONTENTMENT
— FOR THE ROWAN TREES OF AUTUMN

I boundlessly love this new day

today's sun   today's horse   today's rowan trees

make me healthy abundant   fully possessing this life

from daybreak to dusk

ample sunlight

better than all poems from the past

contentment finds me

contentment says "look   at this poet

he is even more content than me"

splitting open my autumn

splitting open the autumn of my bones

I love you, rowan trees

1987

幸福的一日
　　——致秋天的花楸树

我无限地热爱着新的一日
今天的太阳　今天的马　今天的花楸树
使我健康　富足　拥有一生

从黎明到黄昏
阳光充足
胜过一切过去的诗
幸福找到我
幸福说"瞧　这个诗人
他比我本人还要幸福"

在劈开了我的秋天
在劈开了我的骨头的秋天
我爱你，花楸树

1987

FOURTEEN LINES: THE CROWN

The girl I love
girl of the river
her hair becomes leaves on the trees
arms become trunks

although you cannot be my wife
you will be my crown
I will, like the mighty poets of the earth, wear it
use your beautiful leaves to bind my harp and quiver

autumn rooftops, the weight of time
autumn: bitter and fragrant
inducing stones   to bloom flowers like crowns

autumn rooftops, bitter and fragrant
the air suffused by the crowns
bitter fragrance of split-open laurel and almond trees

1987.8.19 night

十四行：王冠

我所热爱的少女
河流的少女
头发变成了树叶
两臂变成了树干

你既然不能做我的妻子
你一定要成为我的王冠
我将和人间的伟大诗人一同佩戴
用你美丽叶子缠绕我的竖琴和箭袋

秋天的屋顶时间的重量
秋天又苦又香
使石头开花　像一顶王冠

秋天的屋顶又苦又香
空中弥漫着一顶王冠
被劈开的月桂和扁桃的苦香

1987.8.19 夜

EARTH· SADNESS · DEATH

Dusk, my flowing blood-stained arteries cannot induce the sheep to
    procreate.
dawn, as if I rise from the womb, like a skinned rabbit on a breakfast
    plate.
night, I tumble down from the stars, castrating or impregnating horses in
    the cemetery.
day, my coffin floats down the river and is pieced together to form this
    bridge or
        marriage boat.

clusters of my bones form rooftops on the water, remnants of humanity.
swallows and monkeys sit in the belly of my wilderness, primal desires.
in my heart the royal court of Chu stoically faces refugees from the north.
now the people of the world ready their rations before war.

at the last supper the food passes right through our young women
their wounds   the seams in their skulls
the last supper is brought before us
together at the feast, impregnated by the crowds: ourselves.

1987.8

土地 · 忧郁 · 死亡

黄昏，我流着血污的脉管不能使大羊生殖。
黎明，我仿佛从子宫中升起，如剥皮的兔子摆上早餐。
夜晚，我从星辰上坠落，使墓地的群马阉割或受孕。
白天，我在河上漂浮的棺材竟拼凑成目前的桥梁或嫁娶之船。

我的白骨累累是水面上人类残剩的屋顶。
燕子和猴子坐在我荒野的肚子上饮食男女。
我的心脏中楚国王廷面对北方难民默默无言。
全世界人民如今在战争之前粮草齐备。

最后的晚餐那食物径直通过了我们的少女，
她们的伤口　她们颅骨中的缝，
最后的晚餐端到我们的面前，
一道筵席，受孕于人群：我们自己。

1987.8

PROCREATION

In the night rain drops down from heaven, falling onto my blue
    eyelids
in the night the gateway to the forest opens wide like a flame
    biting into a thigh
a long maw stretching 10,000 miles across a sea of animals
humans clench their teeth music clearly sounds
in the spreading dense fog of dawn, the wheat of April show its
    heads like a crowd of
        immortals
thunder flashes out 10,000 frogs
a red cart of blood like water flows past pomegranates and
    wombs
the forest cleaves
people hurl abuses feelings break out and run wild
and each constructs a small island where no one stops

I will tell everyone who feels limitless joy in their lives
that their shields left in the caves a thousand years ago are still
    rusting over

1987 (?)

生殖

夜间雨从天堂滴落，滴到我的青色眼皮上
那夜的森林之门洞开若火焰咬在大腿上
一只长吻伸过万里动物的湖泊
人类咬紧牙关　音乐历历有声
四月之麦在黎明大雾弥漫中露出群仙般脑壳
雷声中　闪出一万只青蛙
血液的红马车像水　流过石榴和子宫
林子破了
人破口大骂　破门而出的感觉
构筑一个无人停留的小岛

我将告诉这些在生活中感到无限欢乐的人们
他们早已在千年的洞中一面盾上锈迹斑斑

1987（？）

AUTUMN

Use our bones laid flat on the earth
on the beach write: youth. then shoulder a decrepit father
this time is forever, direction severed
animal-like terror filling up our poetry

whose voice can reach autumn's midnight   reverberating forever
covering our bones laid flat on the earth —
autumn comes.
without a particle of forgiveness or tenderness: autumn comes

1987.8

秋

用我们横陈于地的骸骨
在沙滩上写下：青春。然后背起衰老的父亲
时日漫长方向中断
动物般的恐惧充塞着我们的诗歌

谁的声音能抵达秋之子夜　长久喧响
掩盖我们横陈于地的骸骨——
秋已来临。
没有丝毫的宽恕和温情：秋已来临

1987.8

SUNRISE

At the end of darkness

the sun helps me up

my body like this beloved motherland, blood flowing

    everywhere

I am a completely content person

I won't deny it again

I am complete, I am ultimately content

the ascent of the sun releases my body of darkness

I can't deny the sweeping landscapes of the heavens and this

    country

and her existence...at the end of darkness!

1987.8.30 morning after drunkenness

日出
——见于一个无比幸福的早晨的日出

在黑暗的尽头
太阳，扶着我站起来
我的身体像一个亲爱的祖国，血液流遍
我是一个完全幸福的人
我再也不会否认
我是一个完全的人我是一个无比幸福的人
我全身的黑暗因太阳升起而解除
我再也不会否认　天堂和国家的壮丽景色
和她的存在……在黑暗的尽头！

1987.8.30 醉后早晨

IN AUTUMN

You bring water   grain and a jar of wine

autumn   for a thousand miles around
leaves sleep the earth
fruit sinks into buckets
emitting muted, sad sounds

let our sickles lay down
lush grasslands

autumn waters   rise
up into fruit   fruit
echoing the symmetry of your breasts

秋天

你带来水　　酒瓶和粮食

秋天　　千里内外
树叶安睡大地
果实沉落桶底
发出闷闷声响

让镰刀平放
丰收的草原

秋天的水　　上升
直到果实　　果实
回声似的对称的乳房

autumn   bountiful baskets
heavenly baskets
brimming – "fruit"
the ancient script
of Arabia or the Ganges
carved at the sickbed's head

and the fish are singing   dreaming   villages
water leaves form
leaves hands

echoes
these two bountiful baskets symmetrical
breasts
hands

1986.1 draft
1987.5 revised
1987.9 revised again

秋天　丰收的篮子
天堂的篮子
盛放——"果实"
病床头刻划的
阿拉伯或恒河
的永久文字

而鱼唱着　梦着　村落
水离开了形状
离开了手

回声
这是两只丰收的篮子　彼此对称
乳房
手

1986.1 草稿

1987.5 改

1987.9 再改

AUTUMN

In deep autumn, in the homes of the gods, hawks gather

in the native place of the gods, hawks are speaking

in deep autumn, the king writes poetry

in this world deep in autumn

what should be gained is not yet gained

what should be lost was long ago lost

1987

秋

秋天深了，神的家中鹰在集合
神的故乡鹰在言语
秋天深了，王在写诗
在这个世界上秋天深了
该得到的尚未得到
该丧失的早已丧失

1987

MOTHERLAND
(OR DREAMS AS HORSES)

I want to be the loyal son of distant places

and the transient lover of material substance

like all the poets whose dreams are horses

I must walk with the martyrs and idiots

ten thousand people want to extinguish this fire   I alone hold it high

a huge fire   just bloomed flowers fall throughout the sacred motherland

the same as all poets whose dreams are horses

with this fire I must pass through a lifetime of boundless night

a huge fire   the language of the motherland, and the stones cobbled

    together to construct the Liang Mountain stronghold*

Dunhuang** dreams are supreme—even that July the bones would still

    be cold

like snow-white firewood or hard strips of white snow laid down on the

    mountain of the gods

the same as all poets whose dreams are horses

I launch myself into this fire   and these three are the lantern that

    imprisons me   spitting forth

        radiance

祖国
（或以梦为马）

我要做远方的忠诚的儿子
和物质的短暂情人
和所有以梦为马的诗人一样
我不得不和烈士和小丑走在同一道路上

万人都要将火熄灭   我一人独将此火高高举起
此火为大   开花落英于神圣的祖国
和所有以梦为马的诗人一样
我藉此火得度一生的茫茫黑夜

此火为大   祖国的语言和乱石投筑的梁山城寨
以梦为上的敦煌那七月也会寒冷的骨骼
如雪白的柴和坚硬的条条白雪   横放在众神之山
和所有以梦为马的诗人一样
我投入此火   这三者是囚禁我的灯盏   吐出光辉

10,000 people want to walk across my knife edge   to construct the

     language of the motherland

I am fully willing for everything to begin again

the same as all poets whose dreams are horses

I am also willing to serve out my sentence

of all the gods' creations I decay most easily   with the irresistible speed

     of death

I only truly value grain   I embrace her tightly embrace her   in our

     hometown bearing and raising our children

the same as all the poets whose dreams are horses

I am also willing to bury myself in the peaks that soar around us   to keep

     watch over this serene homeland

facing the Yellow River, I am boundlessly ashamed

my years have passed in vain   I am left with only a body of great fatigue

the same as all the poets whose dreams are horses

time passes by   not a drop remaining   a horse dies in a drop of water

万人都要从我刀口走过　去建筑祖国的语言
我甘愿一切从头开始
和所有以梦为马的诗人一样
我也愿将牢底坐穿

众神创造物中只有我最易朽　带着不可抗拒的死亡的速度
只有粮食是我珍爱　我将她紧紧抱住　抱住她　在故乡生儿育女
和所有以梦为马的诗人一样
我也愿将自己埋葬在四周高高的山上　守望平静家园

面对大河我无限惭愧
我年华虚度　空有一身疲倦
和所有以梦为马的诗人一样
岁月易逝　一滴不剩　水滴中有一匹马儿一命归天

a thousand years from now if I revive on the riverbanks of the motherland

a thousand years from now I will again have China's rice paddies   and

the Zhou*** Emperor's snow mountains heavenly horses galloping

the same as all the poets whose dreams are horses

I choose the eternal pursuit

my mission   is to become a life of the sun

from alpha to omega — "sun" — incomparably glorious, incomparably

radiant

the same as all the poets whose dreams are horses

at last, the gods of dusk lift me into the immortal sun

sun is my name

sun is my life

the corpses of poetry — a thousand-year kingdom and me   buried at the

peak of the sun

riding a phoenix of five thousand**** years and a dragon named

horse — I will inevitably be defeated

but with the sun poetry will be victorious

1987

* Liang Mountain is the location of a famous stronghold in the classic Chinese novel Water Margin. The heroes/outlaws who make use of the stronghold fight against a corrupt government during the Song Dynasty (960-1279).

** Dunhuang is the name of a place in western China where in 1900 a vast hoard of early manuscripts and art, mostly dating from approximately 400-1,000 CE were discovered in man-made caves. Dunhuang was historically a stopover point on the Silk Road and a fertile hub for Buddhist pilgrimage and learning as well as a military and trading center. The discovery has been invaluable for research into classical Chinese religion and culture. Most Chines people are familiar with the site and the significance of the discovery.

*** The Zhou Dynasty: c. 11th century -256 BCE.

**** China is traditionally said to have a history of more than 5,000 years.

千年后如若我再生于祖国的河岸
千年后我再次拥有中国的稻田　和周天子的雪山　天马踢踏
和所有以梦为马的诗人一样
我选择永恒的事业

我的事业　就是要成为太阳的一生
他从古至今——"日"——他无比辉煌无比光明
和所有以梦为马的诗人一样
最后我被黄昏的众神抬入不朽的太阳

太阳是我的名字
太阳是我的一生
太阳的山顶埋葬　诗歌的尸体——千年王国和我
骑着五千年凤凰和名字叫"马"的龙——我必将失败
但诗歌本身以太阳必将胜利

1987

AUTUMN FOR THE MOTHER COUNTRY

The river flow of 10,000 autumns pulling at our skulls   cities plowed by raging fire
our hearts split open each of the wounds born of spring's desires

autumn's distant thunder   sacred fires rage
the mysterious fires of spring turn to ashes falling about our feet

taking along a prisoner, his head jabbering
I will fashion a gold — colored horn from his skull   that is blown in Autumn

he calls me the poet of youth   poet of love and death
in the autumn of the golden horn, he wants me to travel throughout the mother
    country and foreign lands

from Xinjiang to Yunnan   sitting atop 100,000 great peaks
Autumn   like a distant pride of lions   gathering in flight

flying lions of the mother country   carrying me across these sacred cities raged with
    fire
these days the gusts of autumn   blow on my lips of the boundless dusk

on the surface of the earth   each of the desires born of warm trade winds and blood
become corpses and fertilizer   with the golden horn sounding
these days there is only him   forgiving the clamor of all living creatures
wiping the blood stains of spring and summer from our lips
it seems the earth suffers, but is fruitful

秋天的祖国

一万次秋天的河流拉着头颅　犁过烈火燎烈的城邦
心还张开着春天的欲望滋生的每一道伤口

秋雷隐隐　圣火燎烈
神秘的春天之火化为灰烬落在我们的脚旁

携带一只头盖骨嗑嗑作响的囚徒
让我把他的头盖制成一只金色的号角　在秋天吹响

他称我为青春的诗人　爱与死的诗人
他要我在金角吹响的秋天走遍祖国和异邦

从新疆到云南　坐上十万座大山
秋天　如此遥远的群狮　相会在飞翔中

飞翔的祖国的群狮　携带着我走遍圣火燎烈的城邦
如今是秋风阵阵　吹在我暮色苍茫的嘴唇上

土地表层　那温暖的信风和血滋生的种种欲望
如今全要化为尸首和肥料　金角吹响
如今只有他　宽恕一度喧嚣的众生
把春天和夏天的血痕从嘴唇上抹掉
大地似乎苦难而丰盛

AUTUMN DUSK

At the apex of the flame
at the foot of the setting sun
boundless dusk   resplendent and supreme
matures in the sorrow of autumn

sunset earth   huge flames   raging scorched red horizon rolls in
making humans heroic   honored and long-lived   our lanterns
        fragment the dusk
people acutely feel black night's approach 10,000-fold
in hearts eternal language flows

the dust of time   embraces me
bounding in the fire-red hills
no one promised me
a long life or an early death

秋日黄昏

火焰的顶端
落日的脚下
茫茫黄昏　华美而无上
在秋天的悲哀中成熟

日落大地　大火熊熊　烧红地平线滚滚而来
使人壮烈　使人光荣与寿同在　分割黄昏的灯
百姓一万倍痛感黑夜来临
在心上滚动万寿无疆的言语

时间的尘土　抱着我
在火红的山冈上跳跃
没有谁来应允我
万寿无疆或早夭襁褓

on the contrary   this dusk is boundlessly painful
stretching forever   it makes people want to die for sadness
cut open blood vessels
the setting sun deep red

I hope that lovers in the end will become family
I hope that love will last a lifetime
or perhaps   exceedingly transient   and hastily extinguished
I hope that I do not speak of it again

do not bring up the past again
pain and happiness
life does not bring them   death does not take them
there is only the dusk, resplendent and supreme.

1987.9.3 draft
1987 10.4 revised

相反的是　这个黄昏无限痛苦
无限漫长　令人痛不欲生
切开血管
落日殷红

愿有情人终成眷属
愿爱情保持一生
或者相反　极为短暂　匆匆熄灭
愿我从此再不提起

再不提起过去
痛苦与幸福
生不带来死不带去
唯黄昏华美而无上。

1987.9.3 草稿
1987.10.4 改

THE SICKNESS OF STONE
(OR 1987)

The sickness of stone   an insane sickness

an incurable sickness

an incomprehensible sickness

regarded by all marble

as ill stones

used for axes

and the roof over a poor poet's head

to keep him from drifting   across the world

to have him settle down

here, I am the heart of this sick stone

let him live beneath your roof

above your roof of ill stones listen to

bird sounds in early morning just like a lifetime of contentment

the sickness of stone   an insane sickness

stones open their doors budding out homes and poets

seeing how beautiful you are

the stones vie in their illnesses

stone after stone on my body

all of them sick — turning into delicate hearts

that collapse at the slightest blow

石头的病

（或八七年）

石头的病　疯狂的病
不可治疗的病
不会被理会的病
被大理石同伙
视为疾病的石头
可制造石斧
以及贫穷诗人的屋顶
让他不再漂泊四海为家
让他在此处安家落户
此处我就是那颗生病的石头的心
让他住在你的屋顶下
听见生病的石头屋顶上
鸟鸣清晨如幸福一生
石头的病　疯狂的病
石头打开自己的门户　长出房子和诗人看见美丽的你
石头竞相生病
我身上一块又一块
全部生病　全变成了柔弱的心
不堪一击

from a stone-filled wilderness a beautiful woman buds forth

that is the illness of the stones — the illness of all things

how do stones swell open in the dark of the wilderness

these stones will become sick   budding fresh flowers and wine

    glasses

if the stones are healthy

if the stones did not become sick again

where would the flowers bloom

and if I am healthy

if I did not become sick again

my life would be done

1987.10

从遍是石头的荒野中长出一位美丽女人
那是石头的疾病　万物的疾病
石头怎么会在荒野的黑暗中胀开
石头也会生病　长出鲜花和酒杯
如果石头健康
如果石头不再生病
他哪会开花
如果我也健康
如果我也不再生病
也就没有命运

1987.10

MAPLES

Vast day and a night
warm like blood

the trees of frigid autumn in the mountains
a million leaves in a constant wind
warm like blood

in a single leaf we see the coming of autumn
(autumn resides in the north —
a young but robust
flame-lit girl
walking towards maturity and death)

the many, many disasters, many dreams
of women of the northern clans
a sickle and baskets
autumn's heads fall to the ground
sisters' blood stains deep red

枫

广天一夜
暖如血

高寒的秋之树
长风千万叶
暖如血

一叶知秋
(秋住北方——
青涩坚硬
火焰焰闪闪的少女
走向成熟和死亡)

多灾多难多梦幻
的北国氏族之女
镰刀和筐内
秋天的头颅落地
姐妹血迹殷红

women of the northern clans

the autumn of the north, living in its native place

tomorrow's cold sky and frozen earth

short days, long nights

on this long journey our horses lost

women of the northern clans

a fire extinguishing a thousand autumns

fruit is gone but the trees remain

women of the northern clans

— persimmon and maples

plundering each other in this autumn

knife blades flickering

human heads fall to the ground deep red blood stains

an empty cup: the coffin of poetry

warm like the blood of the earth cold as the winds in the sky

1987.11.2

北国氏族之女
北国之秋住家乡
明日天寒地冻
日短夜长
路远马亡

北国氏族之女
一火灭千秋
虽果亡树在

北国氏族之女
——柿子和枫
相抢于此秋天
刀刃闪闪发亮
人头落地　血迹殷红
一只空空的杯子权做诗歌之棺
暖如地血　寒比天风

1987.11.2

FOUR LINE POEMS

1. Longing

Like the wind of this moment
suddenly gusting
I want to embrace you
sitting in a wine glass

2. Star

a tear on the grasslands
contains all anger and humiliation
tears, wandering through all tears
but still only this single drop

3. Weeping

swans like my black hair burning on the lake
I want to bring you to my hometown
two angels sing loud tragic songs
painfully embracing on the rooftops of my hometown

四行诗

1. 思念

像此刻的风
骤然吹起
我要抱着你
坐在酒杯中

2. 星

草原上的一滴泪
汇集了所有的愤怒和屈辱
泪水，走遍一切泪水
仍旧只是一滴

3. 哭泣

天鹅像我黑色的头发在湖水中燃烧
我要把你接进我的家乡
有两位天使放声悲歌
痛苦地拥抱在家乡屋顶上

4. Wild Geese

on green, misty grasslands

a glorious girl

in the place where the moon shines

says   live well, dear one

5.

after the thieves have spoken their last words

they sit alone deep in the night, the dungeon as their orchard

moonlight blows along a thieves' horse

streaming tears

6. Helen

Homer, blind poet

dreaming   of getting that girl

seeing her carrying a glass

using our eyes, we stand before him

4. 大雁

绿蒙蒙的草原上
一个美好少女
在月光照耀的地方
说 好好活吧，亲爱的人

5.

当强盗留下遗言后
夜深独坐，把地牢当作果园
月亮吹着一匹强盗的马
流淌着泪水

6. 海伦

盲诗人荷马
梦着 得到女儿
看得见她 捧着杯子
用我们的双眼站在他面前

AUGUST TORCHES OF THE DARK NIGHT

A vast sun-reddened plain
its shriveled breasts hanging down
like torches in the dark night

people are torches of blurred flesh and blood on these August fields
embracing the harvest in the night
escaping into darkness

warm harvest
rotting harvest
sitting on a torch

1987

八月 黑夜的火把

太阳映红的旷原
垂下衰老的乳房
一如黑夜的火把

人是八月的田野上血肉模糊的火把
怀抱夜晚的五谷
遁入黑暗之中

温暖的五谷
霉烂的五谷
坐在火把上

1987

DAWN AND DUSK
— TWO DOWRIES, TWO SISTERS

Dusk forfeits itself

in the beautiful shades of night

which grow deeper on the mountain peaks

horses and sheep   emerge from the rocks   growing in the mountains

white snowflakes float down through dusk

faintly giving themselves

to me

my secret goddess

what kind of meter should I use

to inform you, to serve you

how should I use my flowing blood

up in the peaks I've licked my wounds

kept watch out over the boundless earth

and taken comfort from this

"forgetting" is my companion

l shall move away from the torchlight that distinguishes faces

and step onto the incurable path

黎明和黄昏
　　——两次嫁妆，两位姐妹

黄昏自我断送
夜色美好
夜色在山上越长越大

马与羊　钻出石头　在山上越长越大

白雪飘落　在这个黄昏
向我隐隐献出
她们自己

我的秘密的女神
我该用怎样的韵律
告诉你，侍奉你
我该用怎样的流血
在山头舔好自己的伤口
瞭望一望无际的大地
以此慰藉

以"遗忘"为伴侣
我将把自己带出那些可以辨认嘴脸的火把之光
从此踏上无可救药的道路

our bodies as the last tents of the grasslands

these mysterious weaving girls

their spinning wheels shined pink by the dusk sky

blood-red axles sounding throughout the night

I submit to these sisters

dying at the sword of sunset glow

flying up through the shades of night

I submit to dusk's secret flight

my body returning to the altitudes of the night

two blood-red halves of the moon embrace

even now

it is difficult for me to say

why those who betray their parents and the homeland

but who ardently love life

will walk this road beside me

my youth my notes on the revolution

engraved by traveling refugees on a beggar's wooden bowl

that once held blood-red sunset colors and our former days

把肉体当作草原上最后的帐篷
那些神秘的编织女人
纺轮被黄昏的天空映得泛红
血液颜色的轮轴　一夜作响

我屈从于她们
死于剑下的晚霞的姐妹
在夜色中起飞
我屈从于黄昏秘密的飞行
肉体回到黑夜的高空

两半血红的月亮抱在一起
迟至今日
我仍难以诉说

那些背叛父母和家园
却热爱生活的人
为什么要和我结伴上路

我的青春　我的几卷革命札记
被道路上的难民镌刻在一只乞讨生活的木碗上
那只碗曾盛过殷红如血的晚霞和往日一切生活

when death comes
does it shatter
or pass down to another child

sunset clouds burn
inescapable misfortune
I am at the limit of life
crying until voiceless, holding to a great poet
but unable to change my fate

I am the poet embraced by others
a treasured poet
I see sunset clouds cast their light upon the grasslands
and my heart feels a special pain

humans like the ashes of dusk and night
scattered at the riverside   sad and exhausted
humans like the feet of kindling   walking the earth

sunset clouds filled with raging flames
and the stench of burning. boundless
stretching out to the plains and desolate beaches
two blood-red halves of the moon embrace
the lonely throne of a poet

在死到临头
他是否摔碎
还是留传孩子

晚霞燃烧
厄运难逃
我在人生的尽头
抱住一位宝贵的诗人痛哭失声
却永远无法更改自己的命运

我就是那位被人拥抱的诗人
宝贵的诗人
看见晚霞映照草原
内心痛苦甚于别人

人类犹如黄昏和夜晚的灰烬
散布在河畔　忧伤疲倦
人类犹如火种的脚　在大地上行走

晚霞充满大火
和焦味。一望无际
伸展在平原和荒凉的海滩
两半血红的月亮抱在一起
那是诗人孤独的王座

I wish that lovers will become family

wish that wheat grows together with wheat

wish that rivers converge with other rivers

vast volumes of river water flow with the shades of the night

the mysterious vagrant king

in the shades of the night returns to his native place

the city smashed to pieces

vagrant king

I sing for you

the shades of the night   reveal the hugeness of the plains   reveals the

    boundless north

       blow this raging inferno everywhere

lifts the immeasurable dusk of the north up into the rolling altitudes

the dawn soars even higher   unfolding over the sea

1987

愿有情人终成眷属
愿麦子和麦子长在一起
愿河流与河流流归一处

浩瀚无际的河水顺着夜色流淌
神秘的流浪国王
在夜色中回到故乡

城市破碎
流浪的国王
我为你歌唱

夜色使平原广大　使北方无限　使烈火吹遍
把北方无尽的黄昏抬向滚滚高空
黎明更高　铺在海洋上

1987

THE SHADES OF THE NIGHT

In the shades of the night

l suffer three times: wander, love, exist

l have three types of contentment: poetry, throne, sun

1988.2.28 night

夜色

在夜色中
我有三次受难：流浪、爱情、生存
我有三种幸福：诗歌、王位、太阳

1988.2.28 夜

IN A VILLAGE IN AN ARABIAN DESERT

Village

And today I am worthless
sitting at the end of this village
this is a moment that keeps no promises
bright starlight on a headscarf
this Arabian desert village now in indistinct dusk
to the east 3,000 miles, the sea
to the west 3,000 miles, snow mountains

Village

March is gone
April is gone
our conversations of last autumn are gone
won't you be my honored guest

in the village – first light comes
on the grasslands – the horses at night are huge
with nothing to say, meeting once, another day

在一个阿拉伯沙漠的村镇上

镇子

而今我一无是处
坐在镇子的一头
这是一个不守诺言的时刻
头巾上星光璀璨
阿拉伯沙漠的村镇已是茫茫黄昏
东面一万里是大海
西边一万里是雪山

镇子

三月过去了
四月过去了
上一个秋天的谈话过去了
请在这个日子光临做我的客人

镇子上——天刚蒙蒙亮
草原上——夜的马很大
少言寡语，见一面，短一日

Village

You sit
on the hillside
you sit on the hillside

living alone in the old granary writing poems
another birthday. an old
horse
flies towards us
an old bolt of cloth
can't wrap this wound

Village

Light the candle
at death we'll meet out on the lakes
just like when we were alive. "Oedipus – the light once shown
on you killing your father and marrying your mother."
candlelight quietly calls
deep green water quietly calls
a blind man sees grasslands and women
— quietly calling in candlelight

镇子

你坐在
小山坡上
你坐在小山坡上

一个人住在旧粮仓里写诗
又是生日。一匹
多年的
马
飞来了
一匹多年的
旧布包不好伤口

镇子

点亮一根蜡烛
我们死后相聚在湖上
宛如生前。"俄狄普斯——光也曾照你杀父娶母。"
烛火静静叫喊
绿汪汪的水静静叫喊
看见草原和女人的一位盲人
——在烛火静静叫喊

Village

On your birthday
you are like a beautiful
female captive
sitting on your hometown's
wheat threshing ground

in the town deep in the night feeling for the door
there was something
l forgot in the mountains

drifter what about you   how can you
wear the bright moon in the water
on your head

horse heads in the dusk
slant toward this village

sisters long ago fell into sleep
at the grain threshing ground   there is no one
there is no one

the sky brightens
the night guard
walks into this mysterious village

1988.5 by deleting

镇子

生日中
你像一位美丽的
女俘虏
坐在故乡的
打麦场上

夜深在村庄摸门
我的什么
遗忘在山上

浪子　你怎么了　你打算用什么办法
将那水中明月
戴在头上

暮色中的马头
斜靠在小镇上

姐妹们早已睡下
打谷场上　空无一人
空无一人

天亮
守夜人
走到神秘的村子

1988.5 删

SUN AND WILDFLOWERS
— FOR AP

The sun is his head

wildflowers are her poetry

l say to you

your mother is not like my mother

under the shine of the moonlight

your mother is a cherry

my mother is tears of blood

I face the sky and say

moon, she is pure dew in your basket

sun, I am the steel on your threshing ground gone insane

the sun is his head

wildflowers are her poetry

beneath an old elm tree

out on the plains

flowing past my bones

太阳和野花
——给 AP

太阳是他自己的头
野花是她自己的诗

我对你说
你的母亲不像我的母亲

在月光照耀下
你的母亲是樱桃
我的母亲是血泪

我对天空说
月亮，她是你篮子里纯洁的露水
太阳，我是你场院上发疯的钢铁

太阳是他自己的头
野花是她自己的诗
在一株老榆树的底下
平原上
流过我的骨头

in the eyes of husband and wife hunters in the mountains
where does that free corpse
drip toward

two mothers in separate places dreaming of me
two daughters in separate places become mothers
while the fields still had lilies, and the sky its birds
while you still had your great bow, a sack full of fast arrows
what should be forgotten, long ago forgotten
what should be left behind, is left behind forever

the sun is his head
wildflowers are her poetry

there will always be days of loneliness
there will always be days of suffering
there will always be days of solitude
there will always be days of contentment
and after, solitude again

在猎人夫妻的眼中　在山地
那自由的尸首
淌向何方

两位母亲在不同的地方梦着我
两位女儿在不同的地方变成了母亲
当田野还有百合，天空还有鸟群
当你还有一张大弓、满袋好箭
该忘记的早就忘记
该留下的永远留下

太阳是他自己的头
野花是她自己的诗

总是有寂寞的日子
总是有痛苦的日子
总是有孤独的日子
总是有幸福的日子
然后再度孤独

who was it who told you this:

answer me

endure your suffering

without a sound

pass through the city

walking from so far away

go to see him   go to see Hai Zi

he is probably even more pained

he writes a poem of solitude and hopelessness

poem of death

he writes:

on the plains

flowing past my bones

the people of the plains   resting beneath elm trunks

like hunters or gods

rising, sitting, seeing each other, and now forgetting each other

sheep and cattle out on the pastures

see the shepherd tumble

down a precipice, blood flowing from his temples

there is no saving him —

he writes:

on the plains

flowing past my bones

是谁这么告诉过你：
答应我
忍住你的痛苦
不发一言
穿过这整座城市
远远地走来
去看看他　去看看海子
他可能更加痛苦
他在写一首孤独而绝望的诗歌
　　　死亡的诗歌

他写道：
平原上
流过我的骨头
当高原的人　在榆树底下休息
当猎人和众神
或起或坐，时而相视，时而相忘
当牛羊和牛羊在草上
看见一座悬崖上
牧羊人堕下，额角流血
再也救不活他了——
他写道：
平原上
流过我的骨头

now, you should

go see him

answer me

endure your suffering

without a sound

pass through the city

that shepherd

may be saved by you

you two could still marry

beneath two great red candles

now he becomes me

in my thorax I will find complete contentment

a red pouch, sheep horns, a bees' nest, lips

and a pair of breasts white as lambs

这时，你要
去看看他

答应我
忍住你的痛苦
不发一言
穿过整座城市

那个牧羊人
也许会被你救活
你们还可以成亲
在一对大红蜡烛下
这时他就变成了我

我会在我自己的胸肺找到一切幸福
红色荷包、半角、峰巢、嘴唇
和一对白羊儿般的乳房

I'll recite poetry for you:

the sun is his head

wildflowers are her poetry

until then   until that night

we can say it another way:

the sun is the wildflower's head

wildflowers are the sun's poetry

they have one heart

they have one heart

1988.5.16 night by deleting from many old poetry

manuscripts from 1986 and later

我会给你念诗：
太阳是他自己的头
野花是她自己的诗

到那时　到那一夜
也可以换句话说：
太阳是野花的头
野花是太阳的诗
他们只有一颗心
他们只有一颗心

1988.5.16.夜
删 1986 年以来许多旧诗稿而得

BLACK WINGS

Tonight in Shigatse, in the first half of the night a light rain falls
only a cluster of northern stars, seven sisters
clenching snow-white teeth, seeing my black wings

seven stars of the north cannot illuminate this world
the herding girl's pillow is highland barley, the place where today she
slept alone tonight has turned to mire
tonight at Shigatse, in the second half of the night the sky fills with stars

deeper into the night is even darker, but not darker than my wings
tonight in Shigatse, I find some bed to sleep on, and hear the cries of an
        infant
how does she feel she has been wronged? is it because she feels the
        contentment of the night

it's alright to quietly sob   but do not go sleepless tonight
my wings, blacker than the night, keep me from sleep
I do not cry or sing praises l want to use these wings to fly back north

back to the north   the north of the seven stars still in the north
pointing the way, like a longing
she grows all over my body beneath candlelight, just like black wings

1988.7 (?)

黑翅膀

今夜在日喀则，上半夜下起了小雨
只有一串北方的星，七位姐妹
紧咬雪白的牙齿，看见了我这一对黑翅膀

北方的七星　　照不亮世界
牧女头枕青稞独眠一天的地方今夜满是泥泞
今夜在日喀则，下半夜天空满是星辰

但夜更深就更黑，但毕竟黑不过我的翅膀
今夜在日喀则，借床休息，听见婴儿的哭声
为了什么这个小人儿感到委屈？
是不是因为她感到了黑夜中的幸福

愿你低声啜泣　　但不要彻夜不眠
我今夜难以入睡是因为我这双黑过黑夜的翅膀
我不哭泣　　也不歌唱　　我要用我的翅膀飞回北方

飞回北方　　北方的七星还在北方
只不过在路途上指示了方向，就像一种思念
她长满了我的全身　　在烛光下酷似黑色的翅膀

1988.7（？）

DIARY

Sister, tonight I am in Delingha, shrouded in the shades of the night
sister, tonight there is only the Gobi

at the end of the grasslands, I am empty–handed
in my pain unable to hold even a tear
sister, tonight I am in Delingha
barren, wild city in the rain

expect for those who pass through or live here
Delingha... tonight
this single last expression of bare emotion.
the single last grassland.

I return the stones to the stones
allow the victorious their victories
tonight, highland barley belongs only to itself
everything's growing
tonight, I am only with the beautiful Gobi the emptiness
sister, tonight I care nothing for anyone, I think only of you

1988.7.25 on a train passing through Delingha

日记

姐姐，今夜我在德令哈，夜色笼罩
姐姐，我今夜只有戈壁

草原尽头我两手空空
悲痛时握不住一颗泪滴
姐姐，今夜我在德令哈
这是雨水中一座荒凉的城

除了那些路过的和居住的
德令哈……今夜
这是唯一的，最后的，抒情。
这是唯一的，最后的，草原。

我把石头还给石头
让胜利的胜利
今夜青稞只属于她自己
一切都在生长
今夜我只有美丽的戈壁　空空
姐姐，今夜我不关心人类，我只想你

1988.7.25 火车经德令哈

THE GRASSLAND NIGHT

A winter pasture

where the grasses grow short and stout

my skull is buried here

embracing these hills in the shades of the night

on the hills the grasses grow the same as last year

as if they never die

the transient summer   beautiful grasslands

are a bride gasping for breath in two blizzards vying with one another

this year's blizzard will come even more vicious

there hasn't been such a blizzard in half a century

my head turns more frigid than the cliffs

a premonition it seems of the doom the heavens have in store for the
grasslands

*

the doom of the grasslands is also my doom

the cows and sheep are all forsaken, none can escape death

only a lame little boy, fleeing to the end of the grasslands

clinging to his horse's neck weeping until voiceless

草原之夜

那是一片冬季的草场
草长得不高，但很兴旺
我的头颅就埋在这里
搂抱着夜色中的山冈

山冈上这些草长得和去年一样
似乎没有经历死亡
短暂的夏天　美好的草原
是两场暴风雪争夺中喘息的新娘

今年的暴风雪会来得更凶猛
暴风雪，五十年未遇
我的头颅变得比岩石还要寒冷
似乎在预感到那天空许给草原的末日

*

草原的末日也就是我的末日
所有的牛羊都被抛弃，都逃不过死亡
只有一个跛男孩逃到草原尽头
抱住马脖子失声痛哭

then the sky became hugely bright
as the sun settled over the entire sky over great desolation
only the lame little boy
clinging to his horse's neck weeping until voiceless

he is my son, already an orphan
his mother, a widow of the grassland she must submit to her fate
my little sister, married off to some distant place
when the time comes to reap highland barley she weeps for me

the other shepherds have gone to the summer pastures
to live together with their sisters or their brides
young people loving life, barley wine flowing in the grassland night
none of them understand my sadness of these moments

1988 (?) .7.28 Golmud

那时候天已大亮
太阳落满天空　　更为荒芜
只有一个跛男孩
抱住马脖子失声痛哭

他就是我的儿子，他已成为孤儿
他的母亲已成为草原的寡妇　　这个女人得会顺从命运
我那远嫁他方的小妹妹
会在收割青稞时为我痛哭一场

别的牧人去了夏天的草场
他们和自己的妹妹或新娘生活在一起
这都是热爱生活的年轻人，青稞酒在草原之夜流淌
他们都不能理解我此刻的悲伤

1988（？）.7.28 格尔木

700 YEARS AGO

The glorious royal city of 700 years ago today is a filthy little village
back then I spurred my horse into the city carrying a sack of highland
    barley
I traded the barley for eighteen human heads
nine remain, buried in the city, whereabouts unknown

in a mountain cave twelve wild beasts dream of becoming hawks, crying
    out in unison
at the mountaintop, the last cave dreams of the heavens
suddenly a feeling, like on the verge of starving walking down this road
in the darkness I write my creed, and the world again becomes light

1988.8.18

七百年前

七百年前辉煌的王城今天是一座肮脏的小镇
当年我打马进城手提一袋青稞
当年我用一袋青稞换取十八颗人头
还有九颗，葬在城中，下落不明

在山洞里十二只野兽梦想变成老鹰，齐声哀鸣
这是山顶上最后的山洞梦想着天空
突然有一种感觉，好像还是在又饥又饿地走在路上
在幽暗中我写下我的教义，世界又变得明亮

1988.8.18

SNOW

With 10,000 sufferings I return to my native place
my snow-white skeleton   no longer grows highland barley

snow mountains, because of your breasts my grasslands brighten
frigid and brilliant

my sickness cured
these days of snow   I only want to die in this snow
the crown of my head emitting radiance

sometimes I lean back onto the grasslands
horse head is my zither   horse tail the strings
l wear the Himalayas a crown of raging fire

sometimes I return to the basin, to lean back onto Chengdu
people have no place here, I have no place here
here there is only love a sword the horse's four hooves

cut off my lips and put them on the fire
heavy snow floating
we no longer see the dirty peaks of yesterday
they are all embraced by snow white breasts

deep in the night   the prince of fire alone eating stones alone sipping
    wine

1988.8

雪

千辛万苦回到故乡
我的骨骼雪白　也长不出青稞

雪山，我的草原因你的乳房而明亮
冰冷而灿烂

我的病已好
雪的日子　我只想到雪中去死
我的头顶放出光芒

有时我背靠草原
马头作琴　马尾为弦
戴上喜马拉雅　这烈火的王冠

有时我退回盆地、背靠成都
人们无所事事，我也无所事事
只有爱情　剑　马的四蹄

割下嘴唇放在火上
大雪飘飘
不见昔日肮脏的山头
都被雪白的乳房拥抱

深夜中　火王子　独自吃着石头　独自饮酒

1988.8

TIBET

Tibet, a solitary rock stretching across the sky
No night can sink me to sleep
No dawn can wake me

A solitary rock stretching across the sky
It says: for a thousand years I have only ever loved myself

A solitary rock stretching across the sky
No tears can turn me into a flower
No king can turn me into a throne

1988.8

西藏

西藏，一块孤独的石头坐满整个天空
没有任何夜晚能使我沉睡
没有任何黎明能使我醒来

一块孤独的石头坐满整个天空
他说：在这一千年里我只热爱我自己

一块孤独的石头坐满整个天空
没有任何泪水使我变成花朵
没有任何国王使我变成王座

1988.8

图书在版编目（CIP）数据

海子诗歌英译选 / 杨四平主编. -- 上海：上海文
化出版社，2023.3
（当代汉诗英译丛书）
ISBN 978-7-5535-2693-5

Ⅰ.①海… Ⅱ.①杨… Ⅲ.①诗集－中国－当代－汉、英 Ⅳ.
①I227

中国国家版本馆CIP数据核字(2023)第027518号

出 版 人：姜逸青

责任编辑：黄慧鸣　张　彦

装帧设计：王　伟

书　　名：海子诗歌英译选

主　　编：杨四平

出　　版：上海世纪出版集团 上海文化出版社

地　　址：上海市闵行区号景路159弄A座3楼 201101

发　　行：上海文艺出版社发行中心

　　　　　上海市闵行区号景路159弄A座2楼 201101 www.ewen.co

印　　刷：苏州市越洋印刷有限公司

开　　本：889×1194 1/32

印　　张：7.125

印　　次：2023年6月第一版 2023年6月第一次印刷

书　　号：ISBN 978-7-5535-2693-5/I.1038

定　　价：58.00元

告 读 者：如发现本书有质量问题请与印刷厂质量科联系 T：0512-68180628